SIZZLE
the
GRUMPY DRAGON

Written by Jennifer Jordan

Illustrated by Ken Morton

Brimax Books · Newmarket · England

Sizzle the Dragon had a bad cold. His nose was red and he sneezed all day long. He tried to blow fire from his nose. But he could only huff and puff.

"You have a cold," said his friends. "You will blow fire when you are better."

But Sizzle sat on a log and felt very grumpy.

"You can have my blue scarf to keep you warm," said Dinky Dog.
"And my red scarf," said Holly Hare.
"And my yellow scarf," said Fluffy Cat.
Buzzy Bee gave him some honey.
Nutty Squirrel gave him some acorn tea. But Sizzle was still a very grumpy dragon.

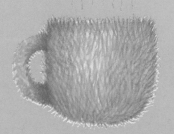

"We must cheer Sizzle up,"
said Dinky Dog.
Every day they told him funny
jokes. Holly Hare stood on her head
and sang songs. Fluffy Cat ran
after her own tail. Buzzy Bee flew
past upside down.
But Sizzle did not smile.
"I have a bad cold," he said.
"I feel very grumpy."

Then Dinky Dog juggled balls in the air. He dropped two and three hit him on the head. Sizzle still did not smile. Then Nutty Squirrel wore a silly hat and made a funny face. But Sizzle was still grumpy.
His friends went away and left him on his own.

The next day Sizzle woke up early.
''Do you know what day it is today,
Fluffy Cat?'' asked Sizzle.
''It is Friday,'' said Fluffy Cat.
''Do you know what day it is today,
Buzzy Bee?'' asked Sizzle.
''Yes, it is Friday,'' said Buzzy Bee.
Sizzle felt very grumpy again.
No-one knew it was his birthday.

"Please can I have my blue scarf
back?" asked Dinky Dog.
"And my red scarf," said Holly Hare.
"And my yellow scarf," said Fluffy Cat.
"I am not better yet," said Sizzle.
But he did not sniff or sneeze
at all. He took off the scarves.
"Now my neck is cold," he said.

His friends had a lot of work
to do. Sizzle was too grumpy to help,
so he sat under a tree. He saw
Dinky Dog collecting wood.
Then Holly Hare made a big pile
of leaves. Fluffy Cat helped
Nutty Squirrel to carry some boxes.
Buzzy Bee buzzed by with some twigs.
Finally, there was a big pile
of wood and leaves. The animals stood
and looked at their bonfire.

"We cannot light our bonfire,"
said Nutty Squirrel.
Then they saw Sizzle under the tree.
"Please light our bonfire, Sizzle,"
said Dinky Dog.
But Sizzle would not even try.
"I cannot blow fire," he said.
"I still have a cold."

But his friends knew he was better.
So Nutty Squirrel took a pepper pot
and climbed to the top of the tree.
He shook some pepper over Sizzle.
"My nose tickles," said Sizzle.
Nutty shook more pepper on to Sizzle.
"Now my nose really tickles,"
said Sizzle.

Then Sizzle gave a very, very big
sneeze. A-A-A-TISHOOO!
Fire and smoke blew from his nose.
It blew through the trees
and lit the bonfire.
"Well done, Sizzle," said his friends.
"We knew your cold was better."
But Sizzle was still grumpy.
"It is my birthday," he said.
But no-one heard him.

Then he saw Dinky Dog's blue scarf.
And Holly Hare's red scarf.
And Fluffy Cat's yellow scarf.
They were hanging from the trees.
They had HAPPY BIRTHDAY SIZZLE!
on them, in big letters.
''You knew it was my birthday
all the time!'' said Sizzle.

"We are going to have a party,"
said Buzzy Bee.
They had hot food cooked on the
fire. They danced and played games
until it was very late. Sizzle had
a lot of fun.
"I will never be grumpy again,"
he said. "From now on I will smile
all the time."

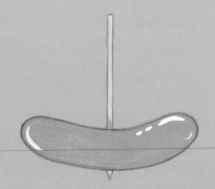

Fluffy Cat made a big birthday cake.
"Now your cold is better, you can light the candles," she said.
Sizzle blew fire from his nose and lit all six candles.
"Happy birthday, dear Sizzle, happy birthday to you!" sang his friends.
Sizzle smiled. He was a very happy dragon indeed!

Say these words again.

grumpy	funny
sneeze	tree
twigs	smiled
nose	pepper
tickles	honey
candles	jokes
yellow	blow